OTHER BOOKS BY

DANIEL KENNEY

The Beef Jerky Gang

Curial Diggs And The Search For The Romanov Dolls

Dart Guns At Dawn

Lunchmeat Lenny 6th Grade Crime Boss

Middle Squad

The Math Inspectors 1

The Math Inspectors 2

Tales Of A Pirate Ninja

Visit DanielKenney.com where parents can sign up to receive

his newsletter and a FREE story.

The Big Life of Remi Muldoon

By

DANIEL KENNEY

Published by Lyndon Press

TABLE OF CONTENTS

CHAPTER ONE

My name is Remi and from my picture, you probably think this is a story about how I became the world's most handsome kid.

Well...you would be wrong. This is actually a story about how I'm special. Now before you go throwing up in your mouth, I'll have you know I'm NOT the one who started calling me special. That would be my mom whose job it is to pretty much EMBARASS me constantly.

Mom said this whole SPECIAL thing started when she was pregnant. Apparently, her belly got huge, way bigger than most other pregnant ladies. But Mom just figured she was having triplets or possibly even a hippopotamus.

Dad overheard our conversation and explained that no, it was just because mom was *eating as much* as a hippopotamus.

I don't think Mom appreciated Dad's comment very much because right after Dad said that, she chased him through the house with a broom.

Well, after the day finally came for my parents to go to the hospital, they had to wait a really long time for me to be born. But the thing is, my dad's not the most patient guy in the world and he eventually got so bored and hungry that, when mom wasn't looking, he snuck out of the room and went down to the hospital cafeteria for a sandwich. And yep, YOU

GUESSED IT, that's when I was born! When the nurse finally brought me over to my mom, I was already smiling. No crying at all.

There was just one problem.

I was small.

REALLY SMALL!

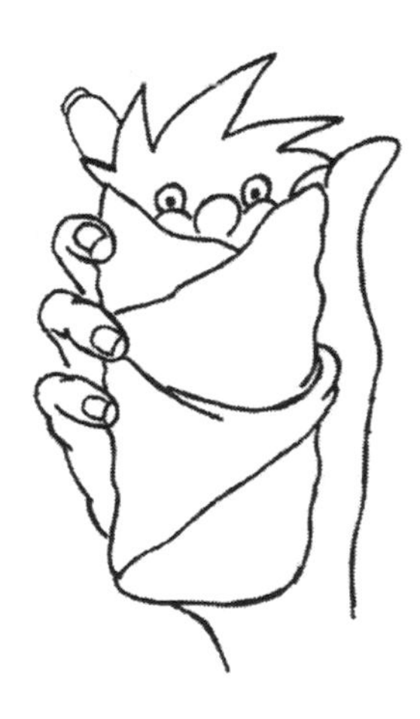

The nurses and doctors had never heard of a baby being so small.

That's when Dad finally came back into the room with his

meatball sandwich from the cafeteria. Mom was holding me up in the air for Dad to see and Dad was so shocked when he laid his eyes on tiny ole me, that he dropped his meatball sandwich right there on the hospital floor. He told me that, at first, he was really sad about losing that sandwich because it was the finest meatball sub he had ever tried in his life. In fact, for a few months after I was born, Dad still thought about that meatball sub because it was so darn good. But, eventually he moved on from that sandwich because he said that I was pretty good too.

Mom told everyone in the hospital that she just knew I'd be *special.* That even though I wasn't as big as a hippo that would be alright because I would be exactly the size God wanted me to be.

So mom and dad decided to give their very small son a very large name.

Remington Winchester Meatball Muldoon

Remington Winchester was an old family name that came from my mom's grandpa who was a very strange dude who loved Remington rifles, Winchester shotguns, but hated brushing his teeth, washing his body, or changing his underwear.

I was named Meatball on account of my dad dropping that awesome sandwich on the hospital floor. My mom says that it was my dad's right to give me one of my names, but she also said Dad was a moron and that he and all his friends come from a strange place called Idiots-ville.

IDIOTS-VILLE
STATE
COLLEGE

CHAPTER TWO

I didn't think much of me being a small kid with a large name until I got into school. That's when I noticed how big all the other kids were.

The three most popular guys in our school were Bumbus, Rumbus, and Ox and even though they were a lot bigger than me, they also seemed to like me quite a bit. In fact, they said I was so cool, that I deserved my very own locker.

And later that year for my birthday, the guys surprised me with the coolest and biggest balloon you've ever seen in your life. It was called a weather balloon and it must have cost Bumbus and Rumbus a lot of stolen lunch money. Ox was even nice enough to tie the balloon to my arm so I wouldn't lose it.

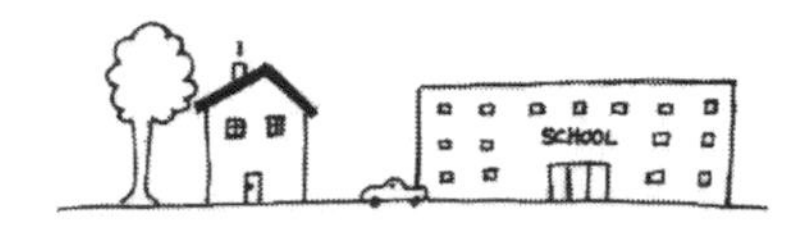

Unfortunately, a strong gust of wind came up just as Ox was kind enough to help me off the top of the playground, and well, I went on a little trip that ended three days later on a pig farm in Iowa.

And then, when the guys heard I loved vanilla pudding, they helped me into the vanilla pudding tub in the school cafeteria. Said they were given me a "pudding bath" since I loved it so much.

I mean, who gets their very own pudding bath? Sometimes those guys were too much.

CHAPTER THREE

When I told my dad about all the stuff the guys did with me at school, he got really upset. He said they were picking on me. I told Dad he was crazy. He decided we needed to see the Great Spirit Man. The Great Spirit Man was a weird car mechanic my dad went to college with. Whenever things were going bad, my dad always went to this guy for advice. So, now it was my turn to go.

As we walked into this guy's auto shop, I could tell this so-called Spirit Man and I were not going to get along. He had Green Bay Packers posters and gear all over the place, and I was a diehard Chicago Bears fan.

And that's when I saw him, the Great Spirit Man my dad had talked so much about.

"So if it isn't Meatball?" he said to me.

He had used the Idiots-ville part of my name which made me immediately suspicious.

"Remi is just fine," I corrected him. "What's your name?" I asked.

My dad patted him on the back. "His parents called him Erwin, but back in college, we called him Toots A Lot, and the name stuck."

I can tell you, based on the next five minutes, the guy's

nickname sure did fit. His garage smelled just like that pig farm in Iowa and I could barely breathe.

After violating the air quality for a few more minutes, Toots finally lit some colored candles and then played music from this guy named Bob Dylan. This Dylan guy was either the worst singer I had ever heard or the best talker I had ever heard. I wasn't sure. Well, right after this Dylan guy said or sang something about *blowin in the wind*, Toots waved his arms around frantically, smiled big, then *broke the wind*, and stopped the music.

"Meatball," he finally said.

"Remi," I corrected.

"Right," he said in a long drawl. "Remi. I need to show you something, something that has been in my family for more than a hundred years. He turned around, grabbed this 'something' off the bench behind him, and brought it to the table where Dad and I were seated.

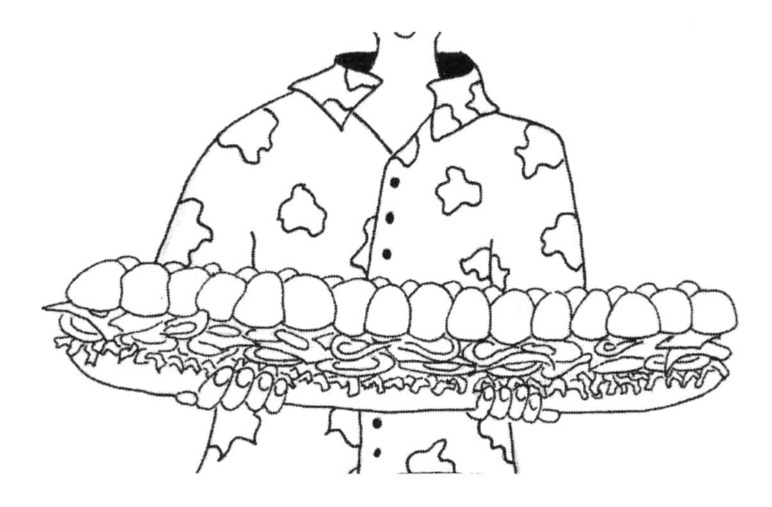

Wow! It was an enormous bun piled with the finest lettuce, tomatoes, ham, and Swiss cheese. I was completely confused.

"Hey Toots, are you saying this subway sandwich has been in your family for over a hundred years?" Because if that was true, then this had to take the World Record for the best looking hundred year-old sandwich in history.

Toots looked down and was so surprised by what he was holding that he dropped that ancient sandwich on the floor. I heard a familiar scream and I'm pretty sure my dad started to cry as well. I'm not sure you can tell, but my dad really likes his sandwiches.

So, while my dad ate party sub bits off the floor, Toots A Lot went back to the bench, grabbed SOMETHING ELSE and came back.

It was definitely NOT a sandwich but it still looked pretty weird. Kind of like a small totem pole, except, instead of sticking out of the ground, it was just resting in Toots' arms.

"Remi, this is the Great Spirit Line. It represents the Spirits of all people that have come before us." Toots laid it on the table and started to examine it like he was a scientist looking at old fossils. Between this guy being a Green Bay Packer fanatic who farted a lot, and my dad crawling around on the floor eating up the remains of a party sub, I was starting to get weirded out. And staring at this funky little pole just made the whole thing even stranger.

Then Toots snapped his head up and smiled.

"Remi my man, it looks like you are special."

There it was again. That word. SPECIAL. Toots A Lot told me that I wasn't *just* special. I had a destiny and that I needed to find people in my life who could help me achieve my destiny.

Destiny say what?

I felt like I was trapped in the Lifetime Channel's version of Star Wars. I was just a kid and all I wanted was for other kids to like me. So, as soon as Dad and I left the repair shop that day, I forgot about Sir Toots A Lot and his Bob Dylan-Obie One Kanobi-mumbo jumbo and focused on something much more important.

My BIRTHDAY!

CHAPTER FOUR

For my 10th birthday party, I planned a huge party. I was gonna show my parents. They didn't understand how things *REALLY* were between me and the other kids at school. I invited all the guys from my grade but I especially wanted my buds Bumbus, Rumbus, and Ox to come. I even sent a few extra invitations to Ox to make sure that he wouldn't misplace his invite.

Finally the big day came. Birthday number TEN. Old double digits. Doesn't get much bigger than that.

There was just one teensy, weensy, little problem.

No one came.

Well, that's not exactly true. This one girl named Frannie showed up. Now, between you and me, Frannie was kind of annoying and to be honest, she and I were *soooooo* different, it made her really hard to relate too.

See, we were absolutely nothing alike. Well, I have to admit, my empty birthday party made me really sad. I did a lot of thinking that night and tried to figure out why the kids at school didn't like me. And I came to a conclusion. I wasn't funny enough. Bumbus, Rumbus, and Ox were always playing jokes on people, especially me. That's why kids liked them so much. So, if I was gonna be popular then I would need to learn how to play jokes.

CHAPTER FIVE

I went to the best joke store in town. Big Mama Jamma's Jokes and Hilarity. Years ago, Big Mama Jama came to our town and turned an old maximum security prison into a Joke Store. I mean, that Big Mama Jama had one terrific sense of humor.

I walked through the aisles and converted cells in amazement. It was the greatest place I'd ever seen in my life. Then a lady came towards me who was bigger than anybody else in the store. This had to be the legend herself.

"Big Mama Jama, is it really you?" I finally asked.

She extended her hand, I took it, and she shocked me with one of those super-secret handshake buzzers.

I think something like a TRILLION volts of electricity

shot through my body. Man oh man was this Big Mama Jama one funny lady. Anyways, when my shorts finally got done sizzling, she asked me what I needed.

I told her I needed to master the art of playing jokes on people. She told me that to become a Master, I would need to learn from the best and dragged me over to the front of the store. She handed me a book. *Big Mama Jama's Book of Jokes And Hilarity.*

"So Big Mama Jama," I asked, "do you mean that if I study

this book, then I will become the greatest player of jokes the world has ever seen?"

Big Mama Jama laughed so hard her belly jiggled. She shook her head. "No," she said. "To become the GREATEST joke expert in the world, you will need my *BIG Book*."

As soon as I laid my eyes on that glorious book, I knew I had to have it. But then I saw the price tag. YIKES! *The Big Book of Jokes and Hilarity* was around one Gazillion

Dollars and all I had was around zero dollars. No way would I be able to afford this book. Not yet at least. I would need to make some money.

And that meant, I needed a job.

Now, my first thought was to go and play football for the Chicago Bears since that had always been my dream, but when I started to study bus routes to Chicago's Soldier Field, my Dad advised me to find something that would be a little easier for me.

"Easier?" I asked.

"You know," Dad said, "something that might take advantage of your, um, special abilities."

There was that word again, special.

At first I was disappointed because I knew the Bears could use a ferocious middle linebacker like myself. But once I opened up my mind, I did some research on the internet and finally came up with a business that I don't think anybody had ever tried before. The next day, I started my new company:

The Loose Change Finding Company.

And let me tell you, I was a natural at this. You give me a couch, and I'll find you enough to take your daughter to McDonald's and still have enough left over to pay me my handsome commission fee.

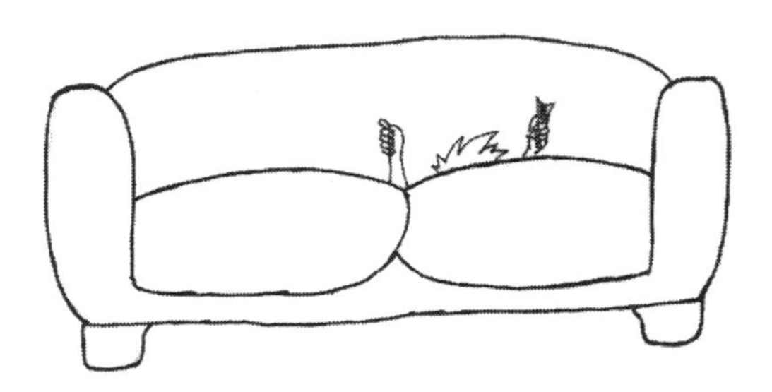

And I wasn't just good at finding loose change in couches. I was terrific at mini-vans, lady's purses, the washing machine, men's wallets, and even the poofy hair of old women.

Well, within a month I had made enough money to go back

to Big Mama Jama's and buy the *Big Book* and get myself a box of rubber snakes to boot.

CHAPTER SIX

For the next week, I spent every moment of free time studying that book of jokes and hilarity. I mean, who knew there were 99 different ways to create a fart smell?

Answer - NOT ME.

Finally, after much hard work, preparation, and sacrifice, I was ready to begin my campaign to become the most popular kid in school. It started off Monday morning after third period, when I managed to fill the bottom of the middle stairwell with whipped cream.

The kids who almost drowned absolutely hated it. But those who tunneled through using their mouths seemed to rather enjoy the experience.

Then, the next day, I rigged the Spanish classroom so that the big weather balloon that flew me to Iowa actually inflated during the middle of Mr. Smith's lesson.

Boy was that funny watching Mr. Smith and the rest of the kids get squished like bugs against the sides of the classroom.

I spent the rest of the week making the school stink, causing people to scream, and generally having more fun than I'd ever had in my entire life.

And to top it off, on Friday afternoon, I pulled my best gag yet. I even came up with a really clever name for it because I was pretty sure I invented this joke.

I called it:

Release Alligators in a Hallway of Kids & Watch Them Scream and Run For Their Lives.

Man, oh man, was that FUNNY! Big Mama would have been so proud. And you know what? My plan worked to perfection. Playing jokes on people finally got me the attention I'd been hoping for. People no longer stuffed me in lockers or taped me to the pop machine.

No sir. I was finally experiencing a little thing called POPULARITY. Now, when I walked down the halls of my school, kids looked at me the same way they always looked at Bumbus, Rumbus, and Ox.

CHAPTER SEVEN

But there *was* a down side to my new found popularity. I'd been working so hard on my pranks that my grades were beginning to suffer. Instead of my usual B's and C's I was now getting some D's and F's.

And Mr. Smith gave me a W. You heard me, a W!

I think it might have been because of that balloon joke I pulled in his class as I'd heard it took Mr. Smith a couple of days to get his face back to its original shape.

In addition to my bad grades, I may have also developed a bit of a bad attitude at home. Well, at least that's what my dad told me.

Dad found me in the basement one day working on my next round of jokes and he asked me to go upstairs and clean my room instead. But I had other ideas.

Dad found it surprisingly easy to refuse my offer and, as a bonus, got super mad at me. At the same moment, we heard Mom scream. Turns out, she had just gotten a call from Principal Munch who was calling to discuss my pranks, bad grades, and bad attitude.

Let's just say Mom and Dad yelled at me a lot that night.

The next day, after I'd already cleaned the entire house for Mom, Dad put his arm around me.

"Remi," he said. "It's time for you to take a good long look inside your Spirit and find out why you were put on this

Earth."

"Oh no," I said.

"That's right Remi, we're going back to see the Spirit Man."

This time I was going to be prepared for Sir Toots A Lot and his Green Bay Packers voodoo magic. I started by putting on my Chicago Bears underwear, pajamas, and jersey as a sort of protective shield.

I figured it would help repel the evil Packers forces inside

Toots' garage.

And I also had a special surprise for Toots that I had worked on all night.

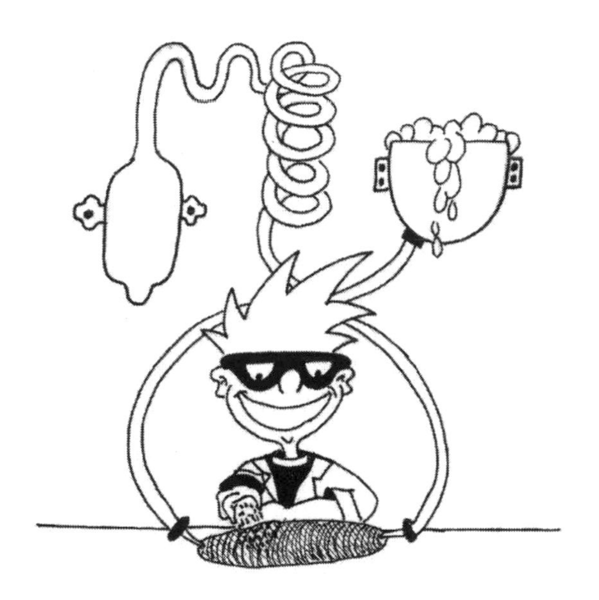

I knew Packers fans were dumb and liked eating big hotdogs called bratwursts so I figured, what better thing to give Toots than an exploding bratwurst?

If right now you're thinking, THAT is the single worst idea you've ever heard in your life, then I really could have used you before I gave Toots his surprise.

When Toots A Lot saw me he said, "Hey Meatball." Then he looked at my Chicago Bears stuff. "I see you're wearing the enemy uniform today."

"You know, Mr. Toots A Lot, just to show you that I don't hate you too much for being a Green Bay Packers fan, I decided to bring you a bratwurst as a peace offering. I've heard it is the food of your people."

"A bratwurst?" he said in surprise as I sat the brat down on the table next to his Great Spirit Line.

I laughed one of those evil genius sort of laughs. "That's right," I said, "and I decided we should cook it right now!"

That's when I pulled out the lighter and lit the end of that brat.

Toots A Lot gave my dad a very confused look, but by then it was too late. The bratwurst was about to go....

When the dust settled around us, Dad grabbed me so I

couldn't get away and then started apologizing to his friend. But Toots A Lot was on his belly, holding the pieces of the Great Spirit Line that now lay SHATTERED in pieces upon his floor.

I mean, was I crazy to think a guy named Toots A Lot who was also a Packers fan would love an exploding bratwurst? Even so, I felt bad. I never meant to hurt anybody or break anything. I was just trying to pull a good gag.

But the damage was done. Dad said I'd deeply dishonored the Great Spirit Man, the Green Bay Packers, and our cultural heritage. I asked if he meant the part of our culture that came from Idiots-ville and that's when Dad grounded me for the rest of my life.

And that night, I didn't learn any new pranks. I just lay in my bed, wondering why God had to make me so darn special.

But I must have fallen asleep eventually, because I had the weirdest dream. I dreamt of the Great Spirit Line, shattered in pieces on the ground, Toots trying to glue them back together—but some pieces—they just wouldn't fit.

CHAPTER EIGHT

The next day at school was pretty rough. I felt terrible for disappointing my mom and dad, and I was really bummed I had spent money on that litter of tiger cubs that I'd never be able to use.

But, I decided it was probably best to stop trying to be so

popular. So, I kept to myself, and just went through my day, like the old Remi used to do.

After lunch, our history teacher Mr. White went to the door and spoke with Principal Munch. I thought I must be in trouble again.

"Class, we need to welcome a new student to our school, "Mr. White said as he finally turned our way. The new kid walked into class and my first reaction was that THIS KID didn't look much like a kid.

First of all, he was tall. Like, freakishly tall for a fourth grader. Secondly, he was wearing the weirdest hat I'd ever seen in my life. Thirdly, this kid had a thick, black beard. I mean, even Ox didn't have a beard.

Wait a second? There was something really familiar about this so-called kid.

"And class," Mr. White said. "Please join me in giving a warm welcome to...Abraham Lincoln."

As soon as Mr. White said it, I slapped my hand to my forehead. OF COURSE! This freakishly tall kid was dressed like:

President Abraham Lincoln!

I laughed out loud and a couple girls turned my way and hissed. But I kept right on giggling. Mr. White wasn't known for his sense of humor but maybe with Remi Muldoon being out of the old prank business, my teacher figured he would step in and start pulling all the gags around school.

That's when Mr. White told Abraham to take his hoodie off, ear buds out, swallow his gum, and take his seat.

The new kid looked at Mr. White and rolled his eyes: "Its Abe old man, got it, Abe."

Now I was *certain* Mr. White was pulling our leg. This was genius! Mr. White must have brought in some high school basketball player to help him teach us a history lesson.

So I waited for the punch line because Mr. White was obviously playing a joke on us. I kept a keen eye on this "Abe Lincoln" character. At first, he squished his oversized legs into his desk, looked around, then put his head down and began to sleep.

In fact, for ten minutes, all he did was sleep. Then, he spent a few minutes hurling spit wads up at the ceiling. When he got tired of that, he leaned back in his chair and began to pick his nose with his pencil.

And that was pretty much it. Mr. White taught the rest of the class in the exact same boring way he did every other day of my life and all Abe Lincoln did was pick his very large nose with a very long pencil. *Maybe the sixteenth President of the United States picking his nose during class was the joke*, I wondered as the last seconds of class ticked away.

Before I knew it, the bell rang, Mr. White dismissed the

class, and that was it. And, as the rest of the kids hustled out the door, I was left staring at a tall kid pretending to be Abraham Lincoln. And all Mr. White did was remind Abe not to come to class the next day wearing his earbuds.

What the heck was going on here?

I went to the drinking fountain, pulled out my portable stool, and got myself a long drink of water.

Maybe I wasn't feeling so good? Maybe that exploding

bratwurst had bounced my brain around so much that I couldn't think clearly anymore?

I kept an eye on this so-called new kid all day long. And there he was, Abraham Lincoln grabbing his macaroni and cheese at lunch. And there he was again, Abraham Lincoln playing with his gum during English class. And then, there he was during gym class, Abraham Lincoln throwing his hat at Becki Glick to get her out during Dodge Ball. And through all of it, nobody paid him much attention. Like he was just any other kid and not at all like he was the

SIXTEENTH PRESIDENT of the United States of America!

Something very strange was going on, and so during study hall I decided that I needed to learn more about Abe Lincoln. I opened up my history text book and turned to the table of contents—to find the chapter on President Lincoln we had studied earlier in the year.

What the heck? The chapter on Lincoln was GONE! Now I was starting to panic. I flipped the pages to where I knew the section on Lincoln should have been.

And...it...it wasn't there. I looked up and then a thought occurred to me. HA HA HA, of course! This was a joke, maybe the most elaborate practical joke in history. I had become so popular, that the entire school had joined together to fool me.

That had to be it. There was NO other explanation.

But...I didn't feel so sure.

Maybe there *WAS* another explanation. Maybe, just maybe, this was a dream. A crazy dream. And if this was a dream, then I needed to snap out of it. I decided to try my old trusty method for snapping out of dreams. I called it

Punching Myself Repeatedly.

After hitting myself 97 times, I was convinced I was NOT asleep and definitely NOT dreaming. That's when I saw Abe Lincoln spit his gum into some girl's hair as she walked by.

I stumbled home that afternoon, barely touched my food, and went to bed early convinced I'd become crazy. And all because of a stupid exploding bratwurst.

CHAPTER NINE

The next morning, my head felt okay, and I figured I wasn't making this Abe Lincoln thing up, so it was time to get some advice.

"Um Dad," I said as he read over the morning paper. "Don't you think it's really strange that our history book doesn't have one mention about Abraham Lincoln?"

My dad pulled his paper down and looked at me with a blank face.

"Remi, is this another one of your jokes?"

"No way dad," I said. "And frankly, I can't believe it either. Imagine, a history book that wouldn't talk about one of the most important presidents in our country's history."

Dad looked confused and shook his head. "I don't know how you came up with the name Abraham Lunkhead, Remi. But I don't find this one bit funny. Not after all the stuff you've pulled lately. I had hoped you already learned your lesson.

Disappointed Remi. VERY DISAPPOINTED."

For a moment, I thought the elaborate joke was continuing. Then, I saw it in my dad's face. I stumbled backwards. Dad was serious. He had NEVER heard of Abraham Lincoln.

The next day, I was wandering in a daze towards math class when I noticed some weird old lady wearing dark sunglasses reach behind Angie Raymond's backpack and steal her math homework.

Angie had no idea. She just kept walking down the hall. The weird old lady saw me staring at her so she took off her shades and gave me a serious evil eye. And that's when I saw it.

This wasn't a weird looking lady.

This was a weird looking DUDE! A dude wearing white old person hair, the way old dudes used to, like even before Abraham Lincoln was alive.

A chill ran up my spine and I got a funny feeling. The same kind of funny feeling I got when I saw Abe Lincoln walk into my classroom the day before. I followed this weirdly dressed white haired dude as he weaved through the hallway traffic and I expected kids to be freaked out. I mean, it's not every day you get a guy this kooky in your school. But here's the thing, he walked through the halls like he was practically invisible. I mean, nobody paid him a second thought. And then, just like that, he was gone.

I didn't see weird dude again until lunch, when I spotted him sneaking up behind Greg Lemon and then watched him steal English homework out of Greg's bag.

This guy was like the great homework thief of the century!

I was standing up to get a better look at him when I heard the two worst words a small kid like me can ever hear in a cafeteria.

FOOD FIGHT!

I turned my head just in time to see Abe Lincoln throw a handful of spaghetti and meatballs across the room.

I immediately dove for cover since the last time we had a food fight, Bumbus had somehow gotten me confused with a sausage burrito and thrown me halfway across the cafeteria before I was stopped midair by Principal Munch's rather surprised face.

I hid under the table as Abe Lincoln continued to chuck spaghetti and meatballs across the room like he was starting a civil war inside our school. As I hid under the table amongst the high tops and knobby knees of the fourth grade, I had time to think. My world was completely collapsing. Abraham Lincoln had just started a food fight in my cafeteria and nobody but me seemed to realize that this was a VERY BIG DEAL! Lincoln was quite possibly the most famous American of all time. But it was like the kids at my school didn't even know who he was! And now there was this weird white haired dude as well. And I just knew there was a *connection* between those two guys.

CHAPTER TEN

I was riding the bus home that day when something hit me hard on the top of my head. As an apple fell into my lap, somebody started whispering in my ear.

"I seen you spying on me kid."

I looked up. It was the dude with the long white hair. He

reached down, grabbled the apple off my lap, and took a big bite out of it.

Another chill ran down my spine. Did he just say—?

"Wait a second, why do they call you Isaac Newton?" I asked.

"What are you some kind of moron?" he said. "That's my name. Isaac Newton. The Sticky Fingers is just what they call me because of my special ability to steal anything, anytime."

I looked at his long white hair and I remembered seeing a picture of the famous scientist and mathematician, Sir Isaac Newton. This kid looked just like that. But maybe that was a coincidence.

Then he took another big chomp out of his apple. Isaac Newton? Apples? The guy from the history books who discovered gravity when an apple bonked him in the head? This HAD to be the same dude.

"You mean, you're really *the* Isaac Newton?" I asked.

The bus stopped, and Isaac and his half-eaten apple stood up to leave. "Just stay away from me kid." He took one more bite and started to follow the other kids out of the bus. As he did, he slipped his hand in Suzie Thornbloom's backpack and stole her homework.

Something very strange was going on and I needed help. I knew Dad was no use since he already told me he'd never heard of Abe Lincoln. But, as my mom had reminded me many times, Dad was from Idiots-ville. Mom might be embarrassing, but when it came to common sense stuff, no one was better than her.

The bus dropped me off at the corner and I walked quickly towards my house. I stepped up to the door, grabbed the door knob and turned—but it was locked.

That was weird. Mom NEVER locked the door. I rang the doorbell and a few seconds later, I heard footsteps, followed by a door latch moving. Then the door opened and there she was.

At first Mom looked straight ahead and then her eyes moved down and when they landed on me, she reacted with surprise. And then something happened that I will never ever forget.

She got a look on her face like she was confused and was trying to figure something out.

"Can I help you, young man?" She asked.

Young man? Well, that was a new one.

"Hey Mom," I said. "Boy have I had a weird day. Think you could make me a sandwich?" I tried to walk past her but she pushed me away with both hands. What on earth!

"Can I help you, young man?" She said again.

"And I heard you loud and clear Mom but I'm really hungry."

Something was off with Mom. That confused look would NOT go away.

"And why are you calling me Mom?" She continued. "Just exactly what is going on here, young man?"

It was right then that it hit me. The YOUNG MAN business. The way mom was looking at me. She wasn't angry at me. Or even annoyed with me. My mom...she...

SHE HAD NO IDEA WHO I WAS!

"Mom, are you feeling okay? It's me Remi."

She held her hand to her face in shock then she turned her head and yelled into the house. "Remington Winchester Muldoon, get down here immediately!"

"Earth to Mom," I waved. "I'm right down here." But she didn't pay me any attention. She just kept her head turned towards the inside of the house until I heard more footsteps and then a new figure appeared at the door.

Holy Buckets of Grapefruit! This kid—he

looked—he looked like me! Well, sort of. He didn't have my prescription goggles, and he was way bigger than me, and he looked angry, and weirdest of all, I think I saw whiskers popping out of his chin. But other than that, he looked just like me.

I looked up at Mom for some kind of explanation but she just patted the kid on the back like she knew him. Like he was her son.

"Remington dear, look how the little tiny kids of the neighborhood have started to dress like you," she said as she talked to the whiskered kid right next to her.

The kid squinted like it was hard to find me. "He looks like a total nerd, Mom," he finally said.

Mom bent down and patted me on the head. "Now run along home to your mommy you small, cute, little boy who doesn't belong here."

I tried to say something but, for once in my life, I was speechless.

Didn't belong here?

There was my mom with some overstuffed version of myself and I was the one who didn't belong?

Mom smiled really big at me and I half expected her to say April Fools or something like that. Instead, she slammed the door shut.

And I put my head down and walked away. Because, clearly, I did not belong.

CHAPTER ELEVEN

I wandered around town aimlessly and did some thinking.

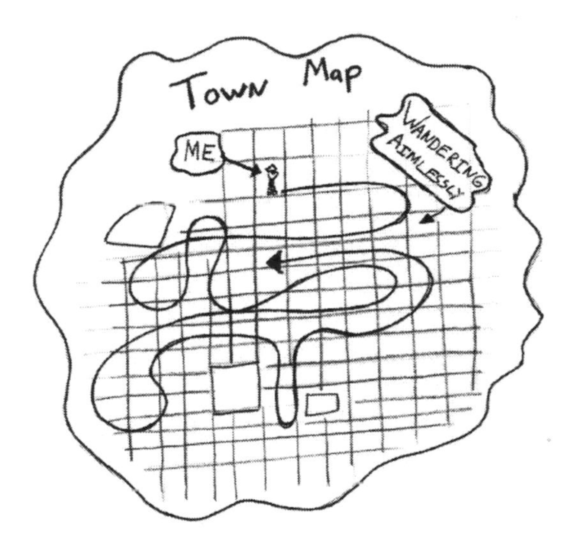

Abraham Lincoln and Isaac Newton were a couple of creeps at my school, and now my own mom didn't even recognize me. She had replaced me with some goon who was a lot more like Bumbus and Rumbus than me.

And I couldn't help but think that, somehow, this was MY fault. All this craziness started after I gave Toots A Lot that exploding bratwurst. The one that blew up his precious—

Wait a second.

THAT WAS IT! Toots A Lot's Great Spirit Line. He told me it included the Spirits of all the people throughout history.

And I had blown it up!

If I had blown up his Great Spirit Line, then maybe, just maybe—I had blown up history.

WHOA!

If this was true, then the only person that could possibly help me had a name that rhymed with Boots Of Snot, and I needed to talk to him right away. I started running, but after a few steps, I stopped and looked right in front of me.

DOUBLE WHOA!

I was already there.

I rushed in the door, Toots saw me, put his hands up and screamed.

"Don't worry Toots," I said. "I don't have anything that explodes today."

He lowered his hands and looked around nervously.

"You're sure?" he said.

"Listen Toots, I'm in big time trouble and I need your help. I think I might have broken history and we need to put your Spirit Line back together as soon as possible or history might be in big trouble."

Toots gave me a funny look. "First of all, I already put it back together. Secondly, what do you mean you broke history?"

So I explained it. All of it. And when I finished, Toots let out a long sigh and blew air threw his lips. Then he farted and it smelled so bad I almost passed out.

"Well Meatball," he finally said. "There's only one thing you can do—

You need to fix history."

"What do you mean?" I asked.

"I'm talking about cracks man, CRACKS! Cracks have appeared in history. I don't know what this has to do with Abraham Lincoln and Isaac Newton, but you're right, they're not acting the way they should, the way history expects them to act. And then there's the matter of that replacement back at your house."

I gulped. "My replacement?"

"Don't you see what's going on here Meatball, you're being erased from you own life."

All of a sudden, Toots flipped up his sunglasses and his eyes went all buggy. He shouted. "MEATBALL! Meatball, where you'd go?"

"I'm right here," I said.

"Meatballl," Toots said again. His eyes were darting around and he looked like he was having a panic attack. "Oh no Meatball, where you'd go?"

"I'm right here!" I yelled as I jumped in the air and waved my arms.

Toots suddenly looked at me and laughed. "Ha! I'm just messing with you man. Figured you deserved it for the exploding bratwurst you gave me. But in all seriousness, if you don't find a way to fix history, then you just might get erased. And history?

It will be broken FOREVER!"

CHAPTER TWELVE

So there it was. I, Remington Winchester Meatball Muldoon, had to FIX HISTORY. To be honest, I had lots of experience fixing things because I had broken plenty of stuff in my life. There was the time I accidentally broke my mom's creepy life-sized porcelain doll, Amy. Well, after my bike crashed the side of Amy's face in, I discovered that my junior football filled up the hole perfectly.

Then there was the time I managed to bash in the front end of my dad's old sports car. Luckily, all it took was seven of my fluffiest stuffed animals placed in just the right spot and you couldn't even tell where the damage had been. And, if I might say so myself, now my dad's car was FINALLY cool.

And then, of course was the time I put a huge hole in our front door. But I got so lucky with this one because, it turns out, that creepy doll Amy fit the hole perfectly. My dad didn't notice anything for weeks.

And that brought us to history. I had to FIX HISTORY. And how does one do that exactly? I guess the same way I fixed my dad's old sports car. I just had to remember how it was originally, and then make it as close to the original as possible.

How hard could it be?

I waited out in front of school the next morning and when Abraham Lincoln came up the steps, I jumped in his way. He snarled at me.

"Move it kid," he said.

"No way," I replied.

He stood on one side and I stood on the other. We were like two cowboys, meeting on main street, ready for a gunfight.

"The name's Abe," he said.

"Not really," I said back. "The American people are going to call you *Honest Abe* but for the most part, they will refer to you as Abraham Lincoln, the greatest president in our history."

Abe looked around, then back down at me. "What kind of a fruitcake are you?"

"I know it sounds crazy, President Lincoln, but hear me out. History is all mixed up and messed up and it's my job to fix it."

Abe leaned over. "Bumbus and Rumbus warned me about you. They said you were super annoying. They were obviously right. Now move it before I hurt you." He tried to step around me but I jumped in his way again.

"I don't care what those guys say because you need to listen to me and fast," I said. "Right now you're acting like a punk and the real Abraham Lincoln wasn't a punk. He was the most non punk that ever lived. He was honest, and brave, and a great leader. If you don't start acting like that soon, then all of history will be broken for good."

Abe gave me a peculiar look, like he was thinking about what I had to say. With my boyish good looks and natural charm, I could be pretty convincing.

Then he kicked me so hard that I landed in a tree.

I'll admit, that did not go exactly how I had pictured it. But, with me getting erased from my own life and all, I didn't have time to whine about it. Once I got myself down from that tree, I decided I might have better luck with Isaac Newton so I went into the hallway and kept my eye on the smartest girls in the school. If Newton was going to steal any homework, this would be the perfect spot.

Well, I didn't have to wait long. There was old Sticky Fingers himself, wiggling through the crowd, about to stick his hand into Nellie Whistler's backpack when I burst towards Newton and kicked him in the shin.

"Ouch!" he yelled as he grabbed for his leg.

"Not this time Newton and not anymore. Never again will anybody call you Sticky Fingers. No sirreee, you are Sir Isaac Newton, one of the greatest mathematicians and scientists of all time. You aren't some thieving punk who steals homework. Nope, you are a genius and it's high time you start acting like it, Sir Isaac."

A look came over Newton's face that I recognized because it was the exact same look that came over Lincoln's face just a little bit ago. But I was ready to handle Newton's objections. Unfortunately, he didn't object. Instead, he growled, picked me up in the air, opened up a nearby locker, stuffed me inside, and locked it shut.

Also not as I had drawn it up. It seemed no matter how hard I tried to fix it, history was trying desperately to stay BROKEN.

CHAPTER THIRTEEN

I pounded on the locker door. I yelled through the little vent at the bottom. I pounded on the door some more. I yelled through the vent again.

But no use. Nothing. I spent the next two hours in that

dark locker. And trust me, it was not nearly as much fun as you might think. I must have fallen asleep at some point and it took the loud ring of the end-of-day bell to bring me back to reality. I then heard a rattling of metal and the door flew open. I jumped out and Sheila Geckles screamed like I was a monster in her closet. Then she dropped her books and ran down the hall. *Still screaming, of course.*

I walked outside, sat on the curb in front of the flag pole, and let my head droop into my hands. I was in trouble. If I couldn't convince Abe Lincoln and Isaac Newton to act the way Lincoln and Newton were supposed to act, then history and my place in it would be broken forever.

Another one of those chills ran down my spine.

I don't know how long I sat there. I watched as bus after bus rolled up to take kids away for the day. I listened as the big football game began at the stadium behind the school. I wondered if my replacement Remington might be at that game.

That's when I heard the SCREECH of tires and snapped my head up to see an old red car skid to a stop in front of me. A man and a woman jumped out and I could see by the expression on the woman's face, something was wrong. She was running towards the school, when all of a sudden she stopped and pointed at me. She turned to the man.

"George, it's that boy, Remi. It's Frannie's friend!"

Frannie?

I stood up as the man joined the woman.

"The school called to say Frannie never made it to her afternoon classes," said the woman. "And she never came home. Then we found this note."

The woman held a small crumpled piece of paper but I wasn't following.

"She RAN AWAY!"

"Oh," I said. "Oh. I, um, I'm really sorry,"

"But you're the one we came to find," said the man.

"Me?"

"Yes," said the woman. "We figured if anyone would know where Frannie might go, it would be her best friend."

"I'm sorry," I said. "I don't know who Frannie's best friend is."

The couple exchanged a quizzical look.

"But YOU ARE Frannie's best friend," the woman said.

I stumbled back. "Me?"

"Well, of course," she said. "Frannie talks about you all the time. She says you're the only one who understands what it's like to get picked on so much and she said you're the only reason she can even stand it at this school."

"She said all that?"

"Yes," the man said. "And we really need to find our little girl. Do you have any idea where she might have gone?"

They looked so scared but I didn't know Frannie and I had no idea where she was. In fact, I usually tried to ignore her. And for some reason, she had told her parents that we were best friends.

Maybe I had made a mistake.

"I said do you know where she might have gone?" the man asked yet again.

I snapped out of it. "No, I don't," I said. "I'm really sorry."

"But do you think you could help us look for her?" asked the woman.

Look for her? I didn't have time to look for SOME GIRL. I had myself to think about.

Then I looked at the expressions on the man and woman's faces. They were scared. And that's when I stopped. All they cared about was finding their daughter and all I was thinking about was MYSELF. In fact, maybe I had spent *too much time* thinking about myself.

Frannie's parents needed my help. *Frannie needed my help.* Maybe MYSELF could wait a bit.

"Please Remi, we need all the help we can get to find her," the woman said. "Please?"

"Okay," I finally said. "I'll see what I can do."

CHAPTER FOURTEEN

And that's when I had my brilliant idea. Frannie's parents said they needed all the help they could get and I figured they were right. So naturally, I headed towards the football stadium.

I HAD AN IDEA.

An idea that might just help us find Frannie and maybe help with a little problem at the same time.

The good thing about Abe Lincoln was that, being freakishly tall and wearing a super weird hat, he was easy to spot in a crowd. I saw him in the middle of the students section cheering on the football team.

I wiggled my way through the crowd and tugged on his pants leg. He looked down and his face soured.

"You? Okay, where should I kick you to this time? How about that water tower over there?"

"Very funny, President Lincoln," I said.

"You really ARE the weirdest kid in the world, you know that?"

"Yep, I know that. Or, at least I'm starting to figure that

out. *Here's the deal.* I don't care where you kick me or how bad you hurt me, I need your help and you're the only one that can do it."

Lincoln scratched his chin. "Why am I the only one who can help you?"

"Because, even though you're trying really hard to be a punk, deep down, you're NOT. Sure, right now you're a freakishly tall 4th grader with a bad attitude but that's not who you were meant to be. I wasn't making up that stuff I told you before. You really ARE GOING to be the President of the United States and our country will need you to be a great leader.

"Abe Lincoln, you are not a nose picking, food fight starting punk. You are a great leader and right now, I NEED A GREAT LEADER!"

He smirked. "I'm no leader."

"Really?" I said. "Let me show you something. Only a great leader could get Ox to start wearing those silly looking hats."

"Really?" Abe said.

"Really."

Abe looked around then let out a long sigh. "What exactly do you need my help for?" he finally asked.

"There's a girl from our school, her name is Frannie, and right now, she's gone missing. Her parents are worried sick and we need to find her before it gets dark. I need you to stand up in front of the football fans and get the rest of our school to help us find her before it's too late."

At first he looked at me like I might be kidding but he must have seen I was serious because he seemed like he began to consider it. "You really think I'm the only one that can do this?"

"I know it. The students will listen to Abe Lincoln."

"What do you think I should say?"

"Just be yourself, I'm sure it will be great."

Lucky for us, they had just started halftime so Abe and I climbed down the bleachers and stood on the field facing the people in the stands. Abraham started to say something but nobody could hear him. Then he put his fingers into his mouth and whistled loudly. The crowd shut up at once. He cleared his throat, stuck his thumbs inside his sweatshirt and started to speak in a clear, loud voice.

FOUR DAYS AND Seven Minutes AGO
YOUR SCHOOL Brought forth a NEW Student... ME!
Now I'LL ADMIT, I'VE Been Kind of a PUNK, ALTHOUGH THAT FOOD FIGHT WAS EPIC!

BUT NOW, ONE of our OWN, MANNY, He NEEDS OUR HELP!
It's actually a girl and her name is FRANNIE

When he finished, there was dead silence and I suddenly got worried that this had been a really bad idea. Then, a boy stood up, pumped his fist in the air and shouted:

FOR MANNY!

CHAPTER FIFTEEN

The crowd walked out of the stadium shouting MANNY, MANNY, MANNY! I wanted to correct them but at this point, it didn't much matter who *they thought* they were looking for. I was just thankful for the help. We went behind the football field into the woods and the meadows that bordered the river. Abe Lincoln led, I was right next to him, and a big chunk of our student body followed, eyes on the lookout for any sign of Manny. Frannie. WHATEVER!

We searched for the next thirty minutes, covering the fields and trees that lined the river when finally, I noticed a commotion over by an old abandoned factory. Some kids were pointing at a huge smokestack and as I got closer, I heard something strange.

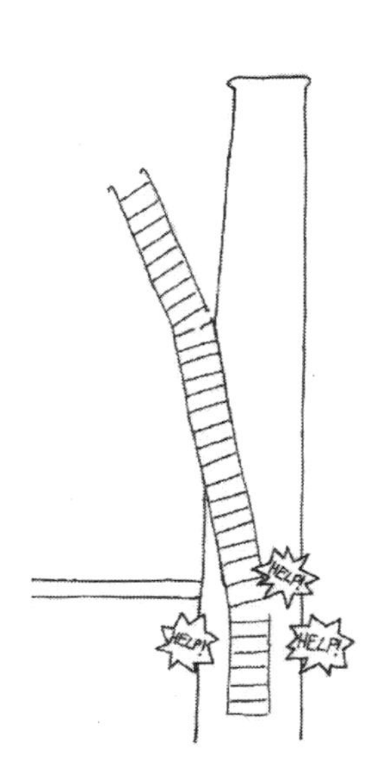

Someone was INSIDE that smokestack yelling for help. I looked at the side of the smokestack where an old metal ladder hung precariously to the side. That had to be it! Frannie must have climbed up the side when the ladder broke, causing her to fall over the edge of the stack and into the deep pit.

Frannie really DID need our help!

"Abe?" I said.

"Already on it kid. Gather round people. We've got our boy Manny in there, he's in trouble and we need a plan for how to get him out. So, who's got a good idea?"

For the next five minutes, the student body discussed different ideas. The worst idea was to wait for an alien space ship to beam "Manny" up and the best idea was to form a human ladder to climb all the way to the top. In other words, all of the ideas were terrible. And that's when the football team jogged up. The football player in front took his helmet off and....

my heart just about stopped.

It was none other than my overstuffed replacement...Remington "Whiskers On His Chin" Muldoon.

A group of girls squealed and a couple of them even swooned. Now, to be honest, I didn't know what swooning was but they were acting so weird I asked what they were doing. And one of the girls told me they were swooning. Then I made the mistake of asking her why.

"Because it's REMINGTON MULDOON

and he's HOT!"

I turned and looked at him. *My replacement was HOT?* That didn't make any sense at all. I mean, this guy looked just like me, well—except for the chin whiskers, big muscles, and grumpy face—and I had never been called hot or cute or anything good in my life. Girls were seriously IMPOSSIBLE to understand.

Remington shook his hair, turned to the group of girls that had gathered and said: "Wasssup?" They practically feinted in response. Then he turned towards Abraham Lincoln. "I'm here to help you find this Lenny guy."

"His name is Manny," said Lincoln.

"It's actually Frannie," I said. "Still Frannie. Still a girl."

Lincoln rolled his eyes at me. "And this Manny, he's stuck inside that smokestack and we need a way to get inside of it and get him out."

"Smokestack?" said Remington as he rubbed his chin whiskers.

Lincoln nodded.

"No problem," said Remington. "I eat smokestacks for breakfast. Let me handle this."

What did this idiot mean, *he eats smokestacks for breakfast*?

Remington walked up to the smokestack while several of the girls squealed HE EATS SMOKESTACKS

FOR BREAKFAST? He knocked on the tall stone smokestack with his fist. He put his ear against the surface. Then he stood back and stuck his thumb out. Finally, he turned around. "I should have a hole knocked in that smokestack in twenty seconds and this Mickey kid out ten seconds after that. Stand back everyone. Then he turned to the group of girls. "And please, ladies, don't try this at home. I'm an expert."

The girls swooned again as Remington put his helmet back on and jogged back about twenty feet. He stomped his foot against the ground.

"What's he going to do?" asked one girl out loud.

"I think he's going to knock a hole in that smokestack," said another.

"But that's impossible," said a third.

"Nothing's impossible for Remington Muldoon," said yet another.

At that, they all swooned yet again and Remington took off on a sprint towards that Smokestack.

I watched my overstuffed double run at that stone smokestack as fast as he could. It appeared that in addition to being big, athletic, and popular with girls, the kid occupying my room was also a complete moron. At the last moment he lowered his head and BOOM! He hit the smokestack and it threw him backwards at least twenty feet.

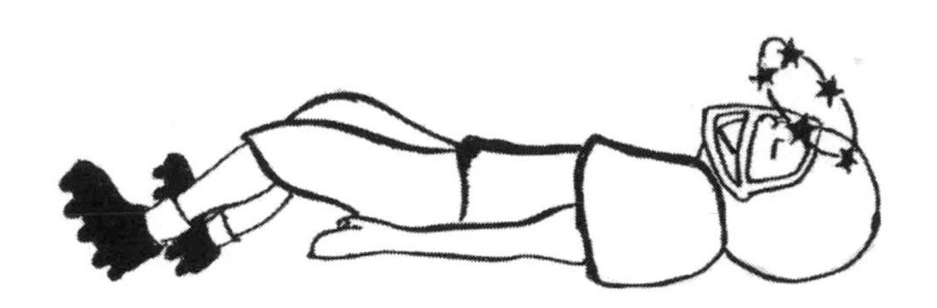

My replacement, Remington Winchester Muldoon, had knocked himself out cold. Two girls knelt down beside him and began to cry.

I gotta admit, it was more than a little annoying to see girls making googly eyes over my replacement. I mean, COME

ONE, the guy looked just like me! So, it was kind of nice to have the overgrown brute out cold for a bit. And now that operation *Knock A Hole In The Smokestack* was officially over, we needed a new plan for rescuing Frannie. I looked up at that smokestack. It was so tall that it looked impossible to get up there. You'd have to be some kind of genius to figure it out.

CHAPTER SIXTEEN

Wait a second! I KNEW a genius. Maybe the greatest genius in history. I looked around, and sure enough, blending into the crowd, stealing something out of some kid's backpack was old Sticky Fingers himself, Isaac Newton.

I ran straight towards him and when he saw me he pointed at me and started yelling.

Not wanting my face broken, I promptly stopped. "I'm not going to kick you in the shins."

"Then just leave me alone, kid!" he shouted.

"Not gonna happen Sir Isaac Newton. Fact is, you've been acting like an idiot who can't pass his classes without stealing other people's homework when the truth is—well, the truth is you're SO smart, you shouldn't even be in our school."

He relaxed a little and shot me a crooked look. "What are you talking about?"

"I'm talking about you and who you TRULY are. And I think, deep down, you know. You know you're smart. And right now, we need a really smart kid to figure out how we're going to get all the way up there and save Frannie."

"I thought we were trying to save a guy named Manny," said Newton.

I growled. "Focus, Sir Isaac. I know it. I know it with all my heart that if you just trusted your brain instead of your sticky fingers, you could figure something out that would save Frannie."

Newton twisted his mouth and rubbed his chin. "Listen kid, I don't know why you think I'm special, but I'm just a regular kid. Sorry to disappoint you."

But I couldn't give up. Not when there was so much at

stake. "THAT is where you're wrong Newton.

EVEN REGULAR KIDS ARE SPECIAL.

They just need to figure out why. Trust me, you can solve this problem."

Newton looked around and chewed nervously on his lip. "You really think so, kid?"

I nodded. "I know so."

"Well," Newton finally said. "I guess I, um, could try."

He tapped his foot against the ground, then shook his head. He walked up to the smokestack, craned his neck, and looked to the top. Then he walked backwards and took a deep breath. Then he closed his eyes and started moving his fingers. I really hoped his plan wasn't to break a hole in the side of the smokestack with his head. But after what seemed like a long while, Newton finally opened his eyes and he was smiling. He ran towards the factory and started busting loose old boards. Finally, he heaved an impossibly large stack of boards, stones, and wires and carried it back towards the crowd of kids.

Newton dropped the stack on the ground and looked at the crowd. "I'm gonna need some help."

At first, nobody moved. Then Lincoln jumped in. "You heard the weird kid with the long white hair, he needs help. Remember, For Manny!"

The crowd roared back "FOR MANNY!" and

everybody hustled over to the big pile. Newton started giving instructions to Lincoln who then handed out orders to the different kids. One kid, a boy named Jeff Davis, didn't like Lincoln telling him what to do so he threw a big tantrum and said he was going home to build his own contraption. But the other kids pretty well listened and over the next twenty minutes, as Isaac Newton worked furiously, something began to take shape. A contraption of sorts.

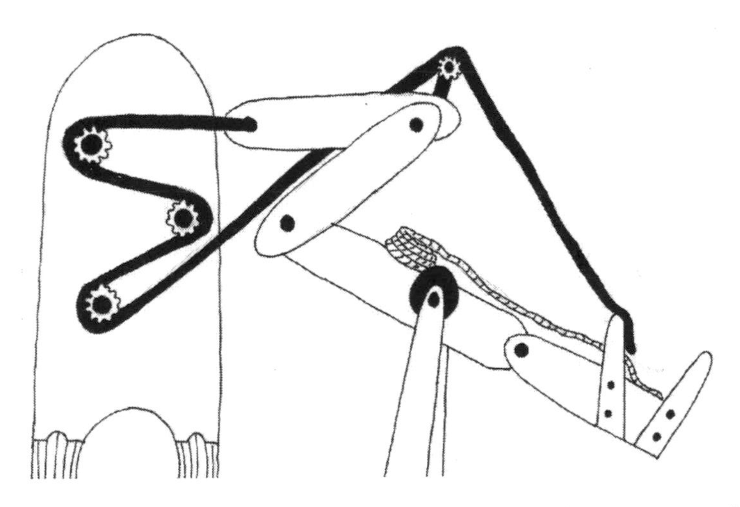

After Newton tightened one last thing on his invention, he looked up at everybody, smiled, and clapped his hands.

"That's amazing," I said.

"You think?" Newton said.

"What does it do?" I asked.

Newton took off his sunglasses and chewed on them. "So um, the general idea is that we will violate the laws of gravity by using this machine to harness the understood properties of motion through space to launch somebody up to the top of that smokestack. Then that person will have to repel down the side of the smokestack, grab Frannie.—"

"Who's Frannie?" asked Lincoln.

"Never mind," said Newton. "Then climb up the rope and zip line back down to the ground."

"Pretty cool," said Lincoln as he walked around the contraption, admiring it. "But it's going to need a name. I've got two ideas. We either call it THE UNION or the Emancipation Pro Contraption. Which one do you like?"

"I was hoping we could just call it the COOL THINGEE," said Newton.

Lincoln clapped his hands together. "That works too. Well, I should probably be the one to ride this baby, seeing as I am the leader of this operation."

"Sorry Abe, not gonna work," said Newton. "For my Cool Thingee to work, I not only need someone very brave, I also need someone who is *very, very small*."

CHAPTER SEVENTEEN

Newton and Lincoln shared a smile, then they both turned my way, funny looks on their faces.

"What?" I asked.

But all they did was look at me with those goofy grins. That's when it hit me.

"Yeah kid, we need you," said Lincoln.

"You need me?" I repeated.

"Yes," said Newton. "You. We need you, Frannie NEEDS you."

And that's when it hit me. This wasn't just about fixing history.

This was about FIXING ME!

I had always wanted to be big, and popular, and athletic, and

NOT wear prescription goggles. And this Remington goofball was all of those things. But, he was also kind of a jerk and for some really strange reason, girls liked him. But right now, none of that mattered. He was knocked unconscious, lying on the ground, and Frannie was *still in danger.*

Only a kid like me could save her.

A KID LIKE ME.

Because, as my mom had always known, I was special, in my own unique way.

I stepped forward, climbed into the Cool Thingee, tied the rope around my waist and received some last minute instructions from Isaac Newton, 4th Grade Genius. Then I looked at the top of that Smokestack.

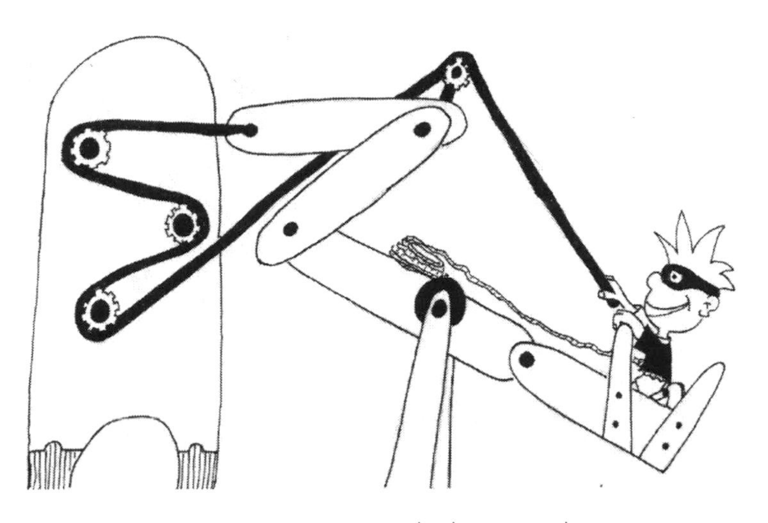

It looked so far away and so high up in the air. I felt my teeth chattering. Then I closed my eyes. *I could do this.* It wasn't about myself. Not anymore. This was for someone else.

FOR FRANNIE.

I opened my eyes, grabbed the rope, and pulled.

The Cool Thingee exploded, hurling me through the air crazy fast and for a brief moment I thought for sure I was going to do a face plant against the side of the stone smokestack and fall helplessly to my death. But, turns out this Isaac Newton kid really WAS A GENIUS. I sailed through the air on a perfect arc so that I was able to clear the front lip of the smokestack and then fall into the very center of the smokestack hole. Then, I dropped through the smokestack until the rope jerked and I finally stopped—just a few feet from the bottom. And right there, curled up in a ball, crying...was Frannie.

Her eyes about popped out of her head she was so surprised. "Remi?" she said. "Remi, is that really you? But how, why?"

"Doesn't matter, Frannie. Right now, we need to get you out of here."

"But—"

"Let's just say, I needed to find my best friend."

I tied the rope around her waist and together we climbed up the side of the smokestack. I rigged the rope to the top of the stack after I strung it through two metal rings Newton had given me. Then I shot Frannie a quick smile.

"Follow me," I said. Then, we jumped off the top of the smokestack and ZIPLINED all the way to the ground where we jumped off and hit the ground so hard I thought I might pass out. Man it was fun!

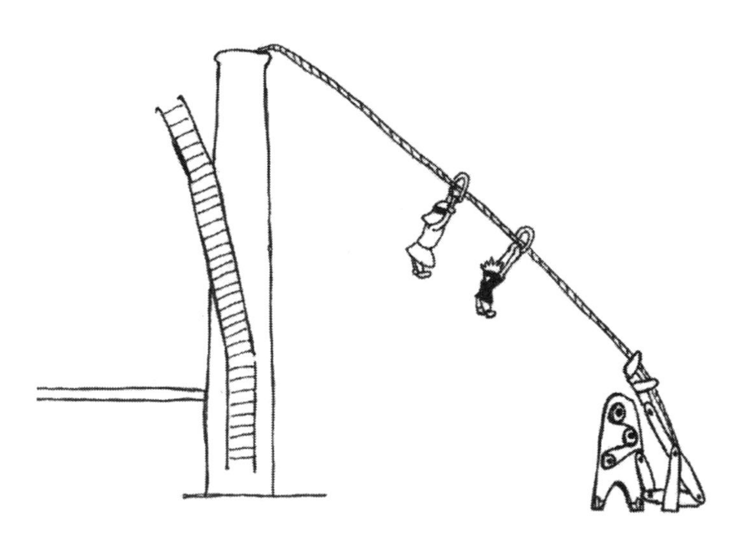

When we stood up, the crowd cheered and started

chanting MANNY, MANNY! Frannie gave me a strange look and I shrugged. "Just go with it okay? Hey, there are two people I want you to meet." I searched the crowd for Abe Lincoln and Isaac Newton so we could thank them for all their help. But I couldn't see Lincoln or Newton anywhere. I asked one of the girls where the new kids went.

"Who?" she asked.

"You know, the tall kid with the funny hat and the weird guy with the long white hair?"

She looked at me like I was nuts, then rolled her eyes, and walked away.

And that's when it hit me. I had done it.

I had FIXED HISTORY!

Then, another thought occurred to me. I ran to where Remington had been lying and as soon as I got there, my heart stopped. He was STILL on the ground.

Something wasn't right. Why would Remington still be there? I had fixed history. I HAD FIXED IT, right? But, if Remington was still here, then the part of history that mattered most to me was still mixed up. Which meant...

I was still being ERASED from my life.

That's when that overstuffed goon started to get up. He stumbled to his feet and took off his helmet. I prepared myself for the swoons and squeals hat would occur as soon as the girls saw him.

But the swoons never came because it turns out that wasn't Remington Muldoon inside of that helmet.

It was OX! It was Ox! It was OX!

I'd never been so happy to see the big jerk face in all my life.

My plan had worked! My plan had WORKED!

CHAPTER EIGHTEEN

Frannie and I ran back to the flag pole in front of our school where her parents were outside speaking to a policeman. Her parents gave her a big hug and, while her mom cried tears of joy, her dad shook my hand and thanked me.

That was the day Frannie Milsap and I became friends. That was also the day I learned that Frannie's last name was MILSAP. That was also ALSO the day I fixed history. And that was also also ALSO the day I ran home, excited to get something from my mom I found myself starting to miss: a big embarrassing HUG.

Well, after I returned to my embarrassing mom and my sandwich loving dad and everything returned to normal, I started hanging out with Frannie. And, believe it or not, Frannie and I really DID have a lot in common. But there were *some* differences. For instance, she did a lot of weird girly stuff. For example, she baked a cake to celebrate the two day anniversary of our new friendship.

Which, of course, is a totally weird thing to do. However, it was also a very tasty thing to do, so I told Frannie she could celebrate our friendship anniversary everyday if she wished.

And believe it or not, Franny and I got along well enough that we even decided to go into business together.

She said it was a "perfect synchronization of strengths that would help us penetrate an otherwise segmented market with a comprehensive business model that took advantage of market inefficiencies."

I, of course, didn't understand a word she said. All I knew is I got to find loose change in couches and eat lots of tasty cupcakes so that was cool with me. I also knew it was a business that took advantage of my ability to squeeze my ridiculously small body into tight and cramped spaces and

Frannie's ability to bake obnoxiously tasty treats. That's right, Frannie's got special abilities and so do I. Turns out my mom was right all along. I AM pretty special. My name is Remington Winchester Meatball Muldoon. A very long name for a very small kid

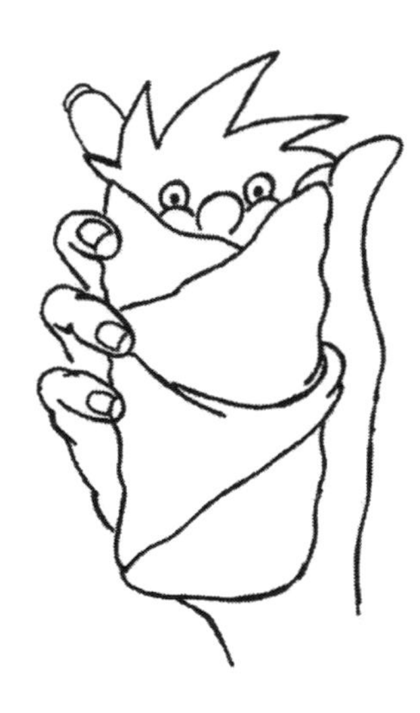

with one very, very

FOOD FIGHT!
SODA
BIG LIFE
BOOM!

CAN YOU HELP ME WITH A REVIEW?

Can you help me spread the word about THE BIG LIFE OF REMI MULDOON? If you enjoyed reading about Remi and his adventures, I would be honored if you asked a parent to help you write a short review about my book where you bought it. Those honest reviews really help readers find my books, and I want to introduce Remi to as many readers as possible. Thank you so much for your help!

WANT TO SIGN UP FOR MY NEWSLETTER?

If you are a parent and would like to sign up for my newsletter to get information about new releases, sales, AND free stories, please visit my website DanielKenney.com

OTHER BOOKS BY

DANIEL KENNEY

The Beef Jerky Gang

Curial Diggs And The Search For The Romanov Dolls

Dart Guns At Dawn

Lunchmeat Lenny 6th Grade Crime Boss

Middle Squad

The Math Inspectors 1

The Math Inspectors 2

Tales Of A Pirate Ninja

Visit DanielKenney.com where parents can sign up to receive

his newsletter and a free story.

DANIEL KENNEY
Story One
THE MATH INSPECTORS
The Case of the Claymore Diamond
Daniel Kenney & Emily Boever
1
Story Two
THE MATH INSPECTORS
The Case of the Mysterious Mr. Jekyll
Daniel Kenney & Emily Boever
2
THE BEEF JERKY GANG
DANIEL KENNEY
TALES OF A PIRATE NINJA
DANIEL KENNEY
LUNCHMEAT LENNY
DANIEL KENNEY
MIDDLE SQUAD
DANIEL KENNEY
DANIEL KENNEY
Curial Diggs
SEARCH FOR THE ROMANOV DOLLS

ABOUT THE AUTHOR

DANIEL KENNEY

Daniel Kenney and his wife Teresa live in Omaha, Nebraska with zero cats, zero dogs, one gecko and lots of kids. When those kids aren't driving him nuts, Daniel is busy writing books, cheering on the Benedictine Ravens, and plotting to take over the world. Daniel is the author of The Beef Jerky Gang, The Math Inspectors, Middle Squad, Tales of a Pirate Ninja, and other fun books for kids. To learn more, please go to www.DanielKenney.com where parents will also have an opportunity to sign up for a FREE story.

Printed in Germany
by Amazon Distribution
GmbH, Leipzig